LIFE IN LAKETON #4

WILDFIRE!

Shawn L. Bird

WATCH FOR MORE BOOKS ABOUT
LIFE IN LAKETON:

1. Back at You
2. After #8
3. Chancey
4. Wildfire!
5. While I Was Out

LIFE IN LAKETON #4

WILDFIRE!

Shawn L. Bird

Flesch reading ease: 88.8
Flesch-Kincaid grade level 2.9
Font: Open Dyslexic

Wildfire!
paperback ISBN 978-1-989642-32-0
ebook ISBN 978-1-989642-33-7
© Shawn L. Bird. 2021
Series: Life in Laketon #4

Lintusen Press
PO Box 10019
Salmon Arm, BC V1E 3B9

to the BC Wildfire Service
& all the fire fighting teams
with thanks

In memory of Ramona,
thank you for my Kilttikoira;
we will take good care of your sweet
Emma.

and my heart dog, standard poodle
Kimelle's Optimum Jive
"OJ"
forever missed

~ 1 ~

"Come on Zuzu!" I called. "Jump! Jump! Jump!" I ran along the row of three dog jumps I'd set up on the dried brown grass of our front yard.

Zuzu, my white standard poodle, ran along behind me, tongue lolling out of her mouth, completely ignoring the jumps. She pulled ahead and stopped short right in front of me, eyes twinkling.

I stumbled, trying to stay upright, but I tumbled over her and collapsed onto the grass.

Zuzu wagged her tail and covered me with kisses.

"Oh, Zuzu!" I laughed, rubbing her curly white coat and soft silky ears as I tried to twist away from her tongue. "You win. It's much too hot for this."

My brother Brian pulled up in his pick-up. His red Wildfire Service shirt was filthy, as were his black pants. He looked over to me as he pulled his duffle bag out of the truck. box "That's disgusting, Delia. You're never going to find a boy who wants to kiss you if you let your dog do that."

I was about to argue that I wasn't looking for a boy to kiss, when the screen door opened, and our mom threw her arms wide for a hug.

"The prodigal returns! How's fire fighting?" She beamed at him proudly.

"It's okay. My crew has a day off since our fire is under control. The mop-up crew is going in now."

Mom looked over at me and scowled, "Get off the lawn, young lady! The neighbours will think we're raising a little hooligan instead of a girl! Go put on a dress and come help me with dinner while your brother has a shower." She turned away from me and wrapped an arm around Brian. "Leave your dirty clothes outside the bathroom door and Delia can put them in the laundry for you." She looked up at the sky and glanced over her shoulder at the dark grey clouds gathering over the hills. "Looks like rain at last. You'd better put away those dog things."

I scowled back at her, but she didn't see me, since she'd already followed Brian into the house. That was fine. I was in no rush to put on a stupid dress and do chores my stupid brother was perfectly capable of doing for himself. Why couldn't he take his own clothes down to the laundry room and put them into the washing machine?

Zuzu nudged my elbow. "I know, girl, I know." I could hear my father's serious voice in my head: 'There are pink jobs and blue jobs. Be proud of who you are!' I pulled myself up and went to gather the jumps. As I approached each frame, Zuzu leapt over it like a deer, just to show me she could jump if she felt like it. She glanced back at me with mischief in her eyes as she landed. "You're a brat," I told her, as she bounded over the next jump before I could get to it.

"Your dog doesn't look very smart. That hair cut is ridiculous."

I looked up to see Chris Turlock from school standing at the road.

"She's probably smarter than you. Her hair cut is five hundred years old, created to protect poodles while they're retrieving game from water. It's a hunting hair cut."

Chris just rolled his eyes. "Yeah, right."

I wasn't going to argue with him. Show poodles have super big hair; Zuzu's is much shorter, in the original ancient style. Shaved bare on the back legs to allow for swimming, but with longer hair for protection over the chest, ankle joints and kidneys. I thought it was gorgeous.

Chris watched Zuzu prancing circles around me before he shrugged and came up the sidewalk toward me. "That's Brian's truck, right? Is he home?"

Zuzu stepped between us and stared at him.

He took another step forward.

Zuzu growled. Her whole body was tense

"Whoa there!" He put out his arms, ready to defend himself if she leapt at him. "I'm not going to hurt anybody!"

I set a hand on my hip and glared at him. "How does she know that after all those insults?" I ran my other hand down Zuzu's back. "Good girl."

In the distance there was a rumble of thunder.

Chris took a step back. "I just wanted to see how things are going with Brian."

"He's just gotten back home. He's taking a shower and then he has to have family dinner. You know how my mother is. She needs to gaze adoringly at her favourite child who is risking life and limb to protect the forests. Do you want me to give him a message?"

"Just tell him I'm on the Volunteer Fire Department now. We're training tonight if he wants to come over and give us any tips."

Brian was working for the Wildfire Service this summer. He'd started as a junior firefighter with the Laketon Volunteer Fire Department when he was fifteen. That gave him training and experience that got him on the Wildfire Service when he was nineteen. It was a dangerous job, but it paid well. I wanted to do it, too, but my parents said it was a 'blue job.'

"I'll tell him." I said, turning away

and hoisting the jump frames onto my shoulder.

"Do you want some help carrying those jumps?"

"Why? Do I look like I need help?"

"Don't be so touchy! I just thought I'd be nice!"

Huge drops of rain began spattering on the ground around us in big drops that bounced on the sidewalk pavement and caused puffs of dust where they landed on the dry ground. We hadn't had rain in weeks.

"I'm perfectly capable," I said, hefting three jumps onto my shoulder. "Go to your training. You don't want to be late."

"You know, if you were nicer, you

might have a better chance of attracting a boyfriend."

What was it with people thinking I needed a boyfriend? I let out an exasperated sigh and spun on my heels. "Come on, Zuzu."

I side-stepped my way past the raised garden beds that filled the back yard and stacked the jumps against the shed, before I walked back to shut the gate. Zuzu was a good girl, but like most standard poodles, she had a mind of her own. If she felt like visiting Horace the Pug or Daisy the Labrador down the street, she'd be out of the yard. She stood waist high to me and was agile enough to climb any fence, so both our five feet of backyard fence and the gate were really just suggestions. Thankfully, most of the time she just wanted to be with me, and both sufficed.

We didn't have an animal control officer in Laketon, and everyone knew Zuzu belonged to me. Still, I didn't want to see her running loose, where she might get hit by a car or picked up by a tourist who didn't know she had a home.

"Delia!" Mom shouted out the window, "quit fooling with that dog and get in here!   We have work to do." She dropped her voice and muttered, "We never should have let you have that puppy."

I smirked. That had been Mom's

constant refrain since I'd saved my money from a summer working at Maggie's Shake Shack to buy a purebred standard poodle from performance lines. I wanted a smart dog to train for agility and obedience and I got one. Sometimes I was afraid Zuzu might be training me more than I was training her, but she was my baby and she made me happy.

The rain was pouring down now, so my hair was plastered to my head and Zuzu looked like a wet mop. The longer hair on her head, neck, and back curled up from the moisture.

We stood under the covered deck, and Zuzu shook herself dry, spraying me. I ruffled her ears and kissed the top of her head. "You're a good girl, Zuzu."

As the backdoor slammed behind us, there was a flash of lightning. Automatically, I began to count under my breath: one thousand, two thousand, three thousand, and then there came the rumble of thunder. The storm wasn't far off.

I walked down the hall and gathered up the pile of clothes Brian had left outside the bathroom, then went downstairs to put them in the washer. When I came back up, Zuzu was turning circles in her basket. She flopped down inelegantly in a tight ball. Brian was in the living room, now wearing his old Laketon High shorts.

Another flash of lightning lit the sky. "I don't like that," he said as the thunder rumbled. "It's so dry out there. Every flash is going to cause a fire that my colleagues are going to have deal with."

Mom bustled in, "We'll just pray that the rain immediately douses any fire started by lightning," she said. "Delia, I thought I told you to get changed for dinner? Did you put Brian's laundry in?"

"Of course." I bit back the urge to roll my eyes. "Can't you hear the washing machine?"

She tilted her head. "Ah. Good. Thank you. Go get dressed."

There was another flash. Brian

opened the front door and sniffed.

"Does anyone else smell smoke?"

~ 2 ~

The next morning, there was definitely smoke in the air.

Brian was standing at the back door, looking up to the hill behind our house eating a cereal appetizer, while Mom busily cooked bacon and eggs for his actual breakfast.

"What do you see?" I asked, blinking groggy eyes. I am not a morning person.

He flicked his chin toward the hill. "There's a plume of smoke. Looks like it's up around Hidden Lake Campground."

Zuzu nudged my knee, asking for her breakfast. While I scooped the dry food into Zuzu's bowl, Mom set a heaping plate of bacon, eggs, hash browns, sausages, and toast on the table for Brian.

"Eat up, sweetheart. You need to get lots of food into you, if you're going to have to go back to work right away."

Brian didn't need a second invitation. He sat down and began shovelling the food into his mouth.

"Where's mine?" I asked.

"You know where the stove is, young lady. Excuse me, while I get dressed." Mom headed off down the hallway.

I scowled after her. "I hate being a girl in this house." I stomped over to the fridge to get out my own eggs and bacon. There was one egg and two rashers of bacon left. "Ah man! This sucks!"

Brian laughed. "Get a plate, she gave me enough for an army. If you're fast, she won't know."

I blinked at the uncharacteristic generosity and brought a plate and cutlery over. He pushed some of his mountain of eggs and a couple of rashers of bacon onto my plate, and settled back into his chair, chewing on his toast.

"Will you have to go back to camp right away?"

He nodded, swallowing. "Probably. I was lucky to get away at all. It's an unexpected break, since those Australian firefighters arrived to help last week." He scooped more eggs into his mouth.

"I'd like to be a firefighter," I said. "It'd be good to feel useful."

Brian started to laugh just as he was swallowing and began choking on his eggs.

I got up and smacked him on his back. "What's so funny!"

He shook his head, wiping tears out his eyes. "You're a girl! Girls don't fight fires."

"That's not true. I know Jan Hollidale's sister was on a fire crew last summer."

Brian rolled his eyes. "The exception doesn't make the rule. Fire fighting is man's work. There is heavy equipment to haul around and it's dangerous in the woods. You can be much more help volunteering to make meals or doing laundry when we come off shift."

"Speaking of laundry," said Mom, suddenly appearing at the table with a stack of folded clothes. I hadn't even noticed her going down to the basement. "Shall I pack this stuff into your duffle for you? I added a few more pairs of briefs and socks, in case you're away from home longer."

'That's great, thanks Mom." He

stood and planted a kiss on the top of her head. At over six feet tall, he towered over the rest of us. "Did you hear Delia's latest brainstorm?"

"What's that dear?" She cast a slightly suspicious look over to me.

"She wants to be a firefighter!" he laughed again.

"Don't laugh!" I said at the same time Mom said, "Don't be ridiculous!"

"Mom, girls join fire crew these days! We're not in dark ages anymore."

"Go get dressed, Delia. I am not even going to discuss such nonsense. Imagine what your father would say!"

I went into my bedroom, Zuzu following along behind me. I knew exactly what my father would say. In his most conciliatory voice he'd say, "Why would you want to do a man's job, Delia? You should celebrate that you are a woman and have other gifts." Then he'd look at me solemnly until I apologized for daring to want to do a 'blue job.'

I hated pink jobs and blue jobs! Everyone should know how to cook for themselves and wash their clothes. Why did my family think only women should do those things? Why can't a woman be a plumber or a carpenter? No reason at all. Lots of women did those jobs these days. But not in my family. My family was positively medieval.

"Come here, Zuzu." I flopped on my bed, and she jumped up beside me. Technically, Zuzu wasn't allowed on the furniture, but I was the one who had to wash the sheets, so who should care whether they were dirty except me?

Zuzu let out a contented sigh and dropped her head onto my shoulder.

"I love you, too, girl." I cuddled her warm body and imagined what it'd be like to be old enough to move away and make my own choices. Three more years until graduation and then Zuzu and I were out of here.

My phone pinged and I picked it up. That was another thing my parents disapproved of. They were sure I was going to be lured into all sorts of trouble because I had a cellphone. They even made me keep it in a basket in the kitchen on school nights. Cheers for summer holidays.

The message was from Chris. "Did you tell him?"

I typed back: "Yes." It was a lie, though. I'd completely forgotten once we started dinner preparations. I pulled on shorts and a T-shirt and went to find Brian.

He was scrolling through his own cellphone in the living room.

"Chris told me that he wants to talk to you."

Brian held up the phone. "Yup. He messaged me. You're a bit behind the times."

I shrugged. "Zuzu and I are going to do some training. Want to watch?"

"Nah. Not my bag, Delia. I like hunting dogs."

"Poodles are hunting dogs!" I told him for the thousandth time.

"Delia. Just give it up."

"I bet Chris wouldn't care if I joined the Laketon Volunteer Fire Department."

Brian narrowed his eyes, "Are you dating Chris now?"

Another rule at our house was no dating until we were sixteen. I still had a year to go.

"Why does everyone think I want to date? No, I am not dating Chris. I simply know Chris because it's Laketon. I want to join the volunteer fire department."

"No, you don't. You are just saying that because Mom said you couldn't. You're being your typical contrary self, little sister."

"Am not."

"Are, too!" he laughed. And then his beeper went off. The piercing tone filled the house.

Mom appeared at the back door, holding one hand over an ear and the other gripping a basket of vegetables she'd just picked from the garden. "Oh, dear! Do you have to go, Brian?"

"Yes. Thanks for breakfast and the clean clothes."

"You're welcome, sweetie," said Mom, setting down a dish of beans. The way she gushed over Brian was seriously nauseating.

"Do you have far to go?" I asked.

"Nope. Just up the hill."

"Oh! That's excellent! Perhaps you'll be home in time for dinner tonight. I'll make a lasagna."

Brian smiled, "That'd be great, Mom, but don't count on it. Looks like this one is going to be trouble. I'll eat with my crew."

"Oh." Mom looked disappointed as she pulled him into a hug.

"I don't mean to scare you," he said over her head, "but this one is close, and the forecast is for wind. It'd be a good idea to prepare a Go Bag with emergency supplies, just in case."

Then he grabbed his duffle bag and headed out the door.

~ 3 ~

Mom watched out the window as Brian drove off down the street. "Your brother is a hero, Delia. I just pray he'll be safe working in those woods!"

"He'll be okay," I said crossing my fingers just in case. "He's got a whole team with him."

Zuzu walked over to the door and rang the bell looped over the handle. I let her out into the yard to do her business. "Do we have an emergency kit ready?"

"No. They're always advertising

that every household should prepare for earthquakes and other disasters, but I didn't think they were very likely. Besides, we're good people. Bad things don't happen to good people."

I knew the Old Testement story about the testing of Job, but I didn't argue with her. Mom was pretty set in her ideas. "Should we put something together? Brian would be upset when he'd warned us, if we didn't listen to him." That was psychology. If I said we needed an emergency kit, she wouldn't do it, but Brian was a completely different matter.

"Yes," she said, drawing the word out thoughtfully. "Brian knows about this sort of thing. We should listen to him. I wonder what we should pack?"

"I'm sure there's something on the internet. I'll look," I said, picking up my phone. "Here, Emergency Preparedness Lists from the official government website." I tilted the screen toward her.

Outside, Zuzu started barking.

"What's got into that dog now?" muttered Mom, glancing out the window.

I handed her my phone so she could see the Emergency preparedness list and went out to check on Zuzu.

"Call off your dog!" Chris called from the back gate.

"Zuzu! Back!" I patted my thigh and Zuzu backed up slowly until she was at

my side. She stared at Chris with one
lip curled and quivering as she growled
under her breath. "She doesn't like
you very much. What did you do to
her?"

"I've never done anything to her!"
He opened the gate and came into the
back yard.

Zuzu growled but didn't move from
her position at my side.

"Good girl," I told her. I rested a
hand on her shoulder. She was
vibrating with alertness. "Brian's not
here. He got paged to go help with
the fire at Hidden Lake."

"Yeah, I know. I'm going up there,
too."

"They let kids go up to fight forest

fires?" I snickered at the expression
on his face.

"I'm older than you."

"By five days."

"You should come fight fires, too.
The department is looking for more
volunteers to help with the Hidden
Lake fire. We don't do the front line
stuff, but we can do less dangerous
stuff to free up the Wildfire Service
people for the tough jobs. The
department is having a meeting
tomorrow. You should come. They'd
probably take you."

Ah man. I'd love to join a fire crew.
How often as a little kid did I sneak
into Brian's room when he was out and
put on his volunteer fire uniform,

imagining I was a firefighter, too? My mother had freaked out when she caught me one day. I shrugged at Chris. "I can't."

"Why not? I thought you wanted to join?"

I really didn't want to go into the details of my medieval family attitude, so I just shrugged again. "Did you want something?"

"Uh." Colour rose up his neck and he shuffled his feet in the dirt. "Not really. I just thought I'd let you know I was going up to help."

"Okay."

"And that they're looking for more volunteers, so you should come sign up."

"Okay." Now I was feeling awkward, too. "Well, thanks for telling me. Don't get hurt while you're in the forest."

He nodded. "No. I'll be careful. See you around?"

"Yeah, okay."

He let himself out the gate and I watched until he disappeared around the front of the house. That was weird.

There was a rustle in the bush on the other side of the back fence that abutted the forest. Zuzu's ears perked up.

"Easy girl."

Our house was on the edge of Laketon. A few blocks west of us was the lake. To the south the highway wound along the edge of the lake and took travellers to the nearest city, an hour away. To the north, the highway led deep into the Rocky Mountains. Behind us to the east was forest. Pine and spruce trees soared eighty feet and more. There was a bit of a guard between the fence and the forest, not quite the width of a two-way road. That narrow stretch wouldn't be much defence if a fire roared down the mountain. Our entire street would be devoured.

I went to find Mom's garden hose and the sprinkler head. I connected them and set them in the middle of the raised beds, set to sprinkle the entire back yard. I know it had rained yesterday, but it was already dry in the bed again it was so hot.

Zuzu stood on her hind legs and tried to catch the spray.

I went inside and Zuzu followed behind. I stopped her at the door and ordered her to shake. She all but rolled her eyes at me as she complied, sending water droplets in all directions.

"Mom!" I called. "I put the sprinkler on the back yard, to moisten things up a bit!"

"It's not our day, Delia! We don't want to get a letter from town council!"

"No one is going to complain, Mom.

The Smiths and the Lords are both out of town!"

Mom emerged from the basement, another load of laundry in her arms. "That's not the point, Delia. We are law-abiding citizens in this house."

"Yes, ma'am. I'll go turn it off."

"Thank you." She headed off to the bedrooms to put away the laundry.

I pushed the door open and let it shut without going outside. The scent of smoke wafted in.

Zuzu tilted her head in enquiry.

I put my finger to my lips. I opened and shut the door again. Let Mom think I had shut it off. I would rather not have our house burn down.

Mom called out, "Delia, pack your

Go Bag. I made a check list. Don't forget you have to make one for the dog, too."

"Her name is Zuzu!"

"I know what its name is, Delia. Pack!"

I took a deep breath and counted to ten before I let it out. "Let's go get your training bag," I said to Zuzu.

She wagged her tail hopefully.

"No, we're not going to agility class today." I took the shoulder bag I used on Zuzu's training days. It had a couple of tug toys, some snacks, a couple of leashes of different lengths, her cooling vest, a portable water dish, and poop bags. I went to the cupboard for an extra-large zip bag and filled it with several scoops of dog food. That would last for a few days. Zuzu wagged her tail again. She loved going places.

"No, Zuzu. Not today." I hung the bag on a hook at the back door well out of the reach of a treat thieving poodle.

Zuzu rang her bell.

"All right, fine." I opened the door.

Zuzu went onto the deck and sniffed the air. Her whole body stiffened, as she stared into the woods on the other side of the fence, then barking madly, she bolted across the wet yard.

"What the heck?" I stepped outside and saw a streak of golden brown moving on the other side of the fence. As Zuzu came toward it, it headed into the woods, Zuzu leapt up onto the frame of one of the raised garden beds, bounded right over the back fence, and sprinted into the forest.

~ 4 ~

"Mom! There's something in the woods! Zuzu just went after it!"

I couldn't believe it. Zuzu loved to race around the agility course, and she was often naughty in class, zooming around the course and not coming when called. At home, though, she usually stayed close to me.

Mom joined me in the yard. We could hear Zuzu barking in the distance. "What is it chasing?"

"I'm not sure. It was low and brown."

"Deer?"

"I don't think so, it didn't really move like a deer."

"Huh." She moved to the fence, which was almost over her head. "She just jumped over the fence?"

I pointed to the raised bed. "She used that as a springboard and just bounded right over! I am going to have to go in the woods to find her."

"It's a dog, Delia. It knows how to find its way home. That's what animals do."

"But there's a forest fire up there! Who knows what could be lurking in the woods!"

"You know very well what's lurking. Deer. Bears. Coyotes. Elk. Cougars. Wolves."

My mouth was suddenly dry. Poodles are smart, and Zuzu looked like a big dog standing at my hip, but she only weighed forty-five pounds. She'd be no match for a wolf or a cougar. "I have to go find her."

"How? Get your hiking boots on and wander aimlessly through the forest? Don't be ridiculous, Delia. It's a dog. It'll come back on its own." She walked back to the house. "Come in and finish packing your Go Bag. You don't want Brian to be disappointed in you."

I stood at the fence staring into the forest where Zuzu had vanished. I didn't care at all about disappointing my brother. I cared about my best friend.

Specks of something were falling from the sky. I looked at the back of my arm where a thin line of grey as long as a fingernail had landed. I touched it, and it dissolved into powder. Ashen evergreen needles.

Brian was the least of my concern. I needed to get Zuzu back home before she was a pile of ash, too.

"Delia!" Mom shouted out the kitchen window.

I whistled the three short blasts that were my signal when Zuzu was supposed to come right away. I listened, hoping to hear branches rustling or barking coming closer. Branches were moving. Wind had picked up and the tops of the trees were bending and dancing in the acrid air. Nothing sounded like it was moving through the undergrowth, though.

I heard a snorting, snuffling bark down the street. That was Horace the pug, down the block. Horace was safely home in his yard where a dog belongs.

I thought, "Zuzu, what were you thinking!" I whistled again, but not even Horace answered this time.

The trees waved as the wind increased.

I needed an action plan. Maybe Mom was right, maybe Zuzu would come back on her own, but maybe something was luring her deeper into the forest and was planning to attack her. Zuzu was fast and she had great stamina, but she wasn't a fighter, despite all the stuffed animals she'd eviscerated in growling, shaking fervour.

I went into the kitchen just in time to hear a buzz as my phone that I'd left on the counter began to vibrate. A musical tone alerted me to a text message. It was from Chris.

"Did you see the news? All of Laketon is on Evacuation Alert."

"What? Why?"

"Hidden Lake Fire is moving in toward town, fast. Go sign up on the Emergency Alert app so you always hear the latest news."

"I will. Thanks!" I set down my phone, heart pounding. "Mom!" I called out. "Laketon is on Evacuation Alert! The fire is moving this way!"

"What?" Mom appeared from the hall where the bedrooms were. "Who told you? Is this just hearsay?"

"Chris texted me. He's with the Laketon Volunteer Fire Department. He knows what's going on."

Mom pursed her lips like she wanted to argue with Chris or the fire or more likely me.

"Let's check the official emergency website," I suggested. "Chris said they also have an alert app; all the official information will be there."

Mom went to the computer and typed into the search engine so slowly I wanted to shove her out of the way to do it myself. "Oh." She said when the page came up. "It's true. It's not all of Laketon, just the southwest half. But we're on alert all right. Oh dear." She took a deep breath. "Your brother was right, wasn't he? I'll move the Go Bags into the car. Have you got yours packed?"

"Not yet. I got Zuzu's ready, though." The thought of Zuzu out in the woods with a fire raging toward her made me cold all over.

"I'll get some water and food packed. You go do your Go Bag."

I stood at the door to my bedroom

and looked around. I didn't know quite where to begin. What do you take when you might never see again whatever you leave behind? I pulled my backpack out from under my bed where I'd stashed it after school ended in June. I dumped out the binders and pens.

What to bring?

Underwear. I would definitely need underwear. I stuffed seven pairs and a couple of bras into the bottom of the pack. Shorts. Pants. A few T-shirts. A jacket. A hat. Jeans. I went into the bathroom and dug around for a new toothbrush and the travel toothpaste. I grabbed chargers and my laptop bag. Then I went into Brian's room and rummaged in his closet until I found the boots he'd worn as a junior firefighter. With a pair of thick socks, they'd be fine for me.

The pack was full. My heart was heavy.

I took the pack into the kitchen, and then took the bag I'd prepared for Zuzu down from its hook. I took both bags to the garage where Mom was arranging things into the trunk.

"Do you have our passports and important papers, like marriage and birth certificates?"

She nodded.

"What about mortgage information and insurance?"

"Not yet. Good idea. We'd

definitely need our insurance information if the house burnt down."

I stared into the trunk. "This is scary."

Mom reached out and gave me a hug. She wasn't a particularly huggy person, but we clung together in the garage. "It'll be okay, Delia. You'll see. If we need to, we'll get somewhere safe."

But would Zuzu?

~ 5 ~

Once the car was packed up, we had nothing to do but twiddle our thumbs and nervously check social media for updates.

We could hear the whir of the planes as they came low, skimming the lake to fill their pontoons with water, to release over the fire. A helicopter rotors thumped as it came low enough to fill its bucket, and then head up the mountain to dump It on the fire.

I wanted to walk down the block to sit on the beach and watch, to get the feeling that I was doing something if only just to observe the firefighters' hard work, but I was afraid of being away from home if the Evacuation Order came.

My first priority was Zuzu, though. I needed to find her. I opened up my laptop and made a poster that said "ZUZU IS MISSING!" Looking through my pictures for a perfect one of her made me cry. I had hundreds of pictures of her. There were pictures at agility trials as she jumped over bars, leapt through a tire, burst out of a tunnel, climbed the A-frame, or raced along the raised dog run. In each photo her eyes were bright with fun and determination. She loved playing in agility. There were also lots of shots of her sleeping in cute positions or posing with new hair cuts. Professional standard poodle grooming is really expensive, so I bathe and clip Zuzu myself each month. Sometimes I intentionally give her a weird hair cut, but lots of the time, they're weird because I screwed up. That's okay. I'm learning. Besides, Zuzu doesn't care. She swaggers like a top model whatever she looks like.

When people see us out walking and ask who does her grooming, they ask if I'll do their dogs, too. So I have a little side business, bathing and shaving down dogs that the owners don't brush properly because when they got them, someone told them they have low maintenance coats. It gives me a few hundred extra dollars each month.

I picked a photo of Zuzu, freshly groomed, her coat gleaming white as she stood, looking alert and happy. I added my cellphone number for contact on a series of tear-offs at the bottom and sent twenty copies to the printer. Then I had to cut all the tear-off slits with the phone number.

"Mom! I'm going out! I'm going to put up some posters of Zuzu."

"Take your phone!" she called back.

I hopped on my bike with a bag full of posters in the little basket I had on the handlebars.

"Nice dog," said a lady as she watched me staple a poster on a telephone poll down the block.

"Thanks."

"What happened? Did someone steal her? I had a friend whose dog was taken by those ladies who cruise through neighbourhoods luring dogs to them so they can take them out of province to sell as bait dogs to dog fighting rings."

I blanched. "Oh! That's awful! Did she get the dog back?"

"Yeah. Someone had spotted the truck and taken the license plate. The police stopped it and seized the four dogs in the back. But they got off eventually with a fine. Not high enough to stop them from doing it again. I always worry when I see a missing dog poster."

I shuddered, "Zuzu wasn't taken. She spotted an animal in the woods behind our house and jumped our fence."

The lady shook her head. "That's rough. Toward the fire?"

I nodded, blinking back tears.

"I hope you find her. I'll keep my eyes out and spread the word."

I thanked her and rode off.

I was putting my last poster up on the bulletin board at the strip mall when my friend Sara came up on her skateboard.

She read the poster. "Zuzu is lost?

That's horrible!"

"She's in the forest. I am afraid she's going to be eaten by a bear or something."

Sara shook her head, "No way. Zuzu is fast. She'd outrun any bear. She'll be okay. And she loves you. You know she wouldn't stay away from you for long. When did she disappear?"

"Last night." I checked my phone. "She's been gone twelve hours." Twelve hours was a long time in the woods. Anything could have attacked her.

"You guys are on Alert, eh?" Sara said.

I nodded.

"It's so scary. Our part of town isn't on alert, but my mom said, 'better safe than sorry' and made us pack Go Bags, too. Kieran was really grumpy about it."

"We've got the car packed, ready if we have to go. I've got Zuzu's stuff, but no Zuzu. What happens if we are ordered out, and she's not back yet?" The thought made me sick to my stomach.

"Where will you go if you have to leave? There are no hotels available because of the tourists who've stayed to finish their holiday."

"I don't know. Dad's out of town visiting my grandparents, and Brian's up fighting the fire, so it's just Mom and me. I don't know what she'll want to do." I brushed tears out of my eyes imagining the fight that was bound to happen. "I don't want to leave until I've got Zuzu, but how will that work?"

"Come stay with us. I've got an extra bed in my room. It'll be like a sleep over. I know my mom won't mind."

"That would be great, actually. I'll ask Mom and see what she says. She'll probably want to talk to your mom and makes sure it's okay."

At that moment, a blaring alarm blasted from my pocket, making us both jump.

"What's that?" Sara said, as I pulled my vibrating phone from my pocket.

"Emergency app." My heart was pounding in my throat as I read the message. "All of Laketon is on evacuation alert now, and my half of town is ordered to evacuate the area immediately."

~ 6 ~

I raced back home where Mom was waiting in the driveway, pacing back and forth. "Where have you been!" she called out, as soon as she spotted me coming down the road.

"I told you I was putting up posters about Zuzu."

She just scowled. "We're on evacuation order, Delia!"

"I know. That's why I came home. I got the message, too."

"I didn't know when you'd be back."

"I had my phone. Why didn't you text if you wanted to know where I was?"

Mom pinched her mouth, because she didn't want to admit I was right.

I held up the phone, showing the flashing red alert message. "It says we have to register at the Community Centre on the other side of town and let them know our plans."

She nodded tersely.

"Hey, can I put my bike on the rack and bring it with me? It'd be good to have transportation."

"I thought we'd just go straight to your grandparents in Victoria. The sooner we get to a ferry the better."

I stood beside my bike. "You can go to Victoria, but I'm not. I need to stay here to look for Zuzu.

"Delia."

"Mom." I clipped the bike rack onto the back of the car and attached my bike into it before climbing into the passenger seat.

"Young lady, this is more important than a dog."

"Zuzu is my dog. You told me that a dog was a serious responsibility and if I insisted on getting a dog, I would be the one who had to keep her safe and healthy. Remember?"

Mom nodded, eyes narrowed. "Yes, but..."

"I promised to look after her the best I can until she dies. So I'm going to find her."

"Zuzu ran into a forest fire, Delia.

It's probably already dead."

A red-hot fury raced through me as we pulled into the Community Centre parking lot. It was full of people milling around nervously.

A volunteer in a safety vest and carrying a clip board came over. "Hi Mary-Beth. Hello Delia. Registration is just through those doors."

Ashes were falling from the sky, like sparse snowflakes.

"Thank you, Carol!" Mom called with a fake smile. She turned back to me. "And where do you think you're going to stay if I were to leave you behind?"

"Sara invited me to stay with them. Their house is just on alert."

Mom gave a snorting noise as she found the line that coincided with our street address. "Just on alert. Fifteen minutes ago we were 'just on alert' and now we're registering with emergency services while we abandon our home!"

"Please, Mom?" I stared at her with all my desperation in my eyes. "I need to find Zuzu."

She rolled her eyes and muttered, "I have to talk to Meghan and make sure it's okay."

"Thank you!" I threw my arms around her. "Oh look! She's one of the registration volunteers. You can ask her now."

When we got to the front on the

line, Mom smiled wanly at Sara's mom.

"Hello Mary-Beth. Scary times, eh?" said Mrs. Smith.

"Hi Meghan. Yes. Incredibly scary."

Mrs. Smith flipped through some papers until she found the one she wanted. "Address?"

Mom repeated it.

"Perfect." She ticked a line on the paper. "How many in the household?"

"Four. But only two to register."

"Oh. You'd better give me the details."

"Robert, my husband is out of town right now. Our son Brian is fighting the fire. He's working with the Wildfire Service this summer. So it's just Delia and me."

"Good." Mrs. Smith winked at Delia. "What are your evacuation plans?"

"I will go to Victoria. That's where Robert is. Delia has lost her dog and doesn't want to leave until it's found. She says Sara invited her to stay at your house?"

Sara's mom smiled. "Yes. She mentioned that. It's absolutely fine with me. Sara has a room with two beds in the basement where it's lovely and cool. No air conditioning in the rest of the house, I'm afraid."

"That's okay," I said quickly. "Thanks so much Mrs. Smith. I really appreciate it."

"Not a problem. All right, I just

need contact phone numbers for you
both?"

She wrote our cell phone numbers
on the form and then took a piece of
scrap paper and wrote a number on it.
"That's everything then. Mary-Beth, if
the rest of town is evacuated, we will
go to Calgary where we have some
family. Here's my number." She slid
the paper across the table. "We'll
take Delia and Zuzu," she smiled at
me, "it won't be a problem. Don't
worry."

"Thank you. That's very kind. I am
sorry she's being such a bother."

"No bother." She glanced past us
and nodded to whoever was behind us
in the line.

"Thanks again," Mom told Mrs. Smith as we left the line and walked back to the car. "I am not happy with this, Delia."

"I know. I'm sorry. I just can't leave Zuzu!"

"Come on, I'll drive you over to Sara's house."

Sara was at their front door and waved as we pulled up. "Yay!" she called, as I opened the car door. "I'm so glad you're staying."

"It was kind of you to invite her," Mom said as she glanced at her watch. "You be sure to behave, Delia."

"I always behave!"

"You, too, Sara," she added.

Sara blushed. "I'll do my best,

ma'am," she said as she took my bag.

I lifted the bike off the rack. "I should keep the bike rack, in case we need to evacuate from here, too."

Mom just sighed as I undid the straps and clips, but before I was ready, she reached for my shoulder and pulled me into a hug. "You be careful! Don't do anything stupid while you're looking for that dog. I love you."

"I love you, too. Mom. Say hi to dad and Grandma and Grandpa."

She nodded, sniffing and blinking. She climbed back into the car, waving as she pulled out of the driveway. She had a five-hour drive to the ferry.

It was weird being left.

Sara threw an arm around my shoulder. Come on. Leave the bike and rack there in the corner."

We walked into the house. It was hot inside, but the air was considerably fresher than it was outside. I hadn't really noticed the smoke as we were in it, but now we were inside I started to cough.

"Hi, Delia," said Sara's brother Kieran as we walked past the living room where he was playing some game on his phone.

I nodded a greeting. We were still on the basement stairs when my phone rang. I didn't recognize the number.

"Hi." said a deep male voice. "Are you the one that lost the big poodle?"

My breath caught. "Yes! Have you seen her? Do you have her? Is she all right?"

"I don't have her, sorry."

"Oh." My heart plummeted into my belly.

"But I think I've seen her. I am on the fire crew. I was driving out when I saw a flash of white in the trees. At first, I thought it was a deer, but as I was driving out, I was thinking it was too small and light coloured. I just saw your poster. It makes sense that it was your dog."

"That's great! Can you tell me exactly where?" I could ride my bike up the forest road with one of Zuzu's leashes. She could run out. Or maybe this guy would drive me up.

"About the seven-kilometre marker, I'd say."

"Could you take me up there?"

"Sorry. You can't go up there right now. They are moving the crews because the fire leapt the first line. It's not safe for you. I just wanted you to know that the dog is still out there."

"Oh. All right. Thank you for calling."

If it wasn't safe for me in the woods, it sure wasn't safe for Zuzu.

~ 7 ~

The next afternoon the sky was brown with acrid smoke that burned the eyes and throat. Sara, Kieran and I were sitting in their basement watching a DVD when my phone pinged a text message.

Chris had written, "Where are you?"

"At Sara and Kieran's," I typed back.

"I'm off for today. Wanna go to Maggie's?"

"Why are you off? What's happening with the fire?"

"It's still moving, but we're building a new firebreak and the water bombers are keeping it back while we do. Wanna meet me for a shake?"

"Can I bring Sara and Kieran?"

There was a long pause before he replied, "Sure."

I looked up from the phone and asked, "You guys want to go to Maggie's? Chris is going and invited us along."

Kieran snorted. "Chris invited me? Right. Sure he did."

Sara laughed, "You're a necessary evil, dear brother. Chris has a thing for Delia. He's been after her for ages."

"He has not!" I yelped.

She just snickered and shook her head. "You keep telling yourself that."

"We are just friends. Barely friends!" narrowing my brows at her. "Zuzu hates him."

"Really? Did he have anything to do with her disappearance?"

"No, she leapt that fence of her own volition, and it definitely wasn't Chris who taunted her from the woods." I looked back at the phone. Chris had texted me a question mark. "Shall we go?"

Sara stood up, "Of course. Come on, brother mine. Come watch Chris attempt to capture Delia's heart."

"Should be good for a laugh," he said.

"You two both be nice," I glared at them. "Or none of us will go."

Kieran just grinned. "Tell him we'll meet him there in ten minutes. We should probably put on masks, though. The smoke is really thick out there."

We walked up Larch Street to Maggie's Shake Shack in our masks.

"Do you still work at Maggie's, Delia?" asked Kieran.

"Sometimes. I was full-time last summer, but I just wanted a few hours this year. They mostly call me when someone doesn't show up. I have been doing mobile dog grooming, too."

"Oh right! I heard someone talking about that in the Bargain store once. You go to their house?"

I nodded, "Yeah. I had to get this expensive equipment so I can groom Zuzu, so I just added people when they asked. I have a bag of stuff I put in the basket of my bike and do the grooming at their house. People pay in cash." I shrugged.

"How much do people pay to have their dog groomed?"

I shrugged again, "Depends. Little dogs I charge fifty bucks for bath, dry, trim."

"How long does it take?"

"An hour or two. The better I know the dog the faster it is. I don't do anything fancy."

"Wow." Kieran stared at me. "You average thirty-five bucks an hour."

Sara punched him in the arm. "You're being rude."

"Why? I'm impressed. The guys working at the dock are happy to make eighteen."

"I would never have learnt if not for Zuzu." I missed her so much. Thinking about her lost in the woods made my stomach twist into writhing knots.

When we arrived at Maggie's, Chris was sitting at a picnic table out front. He greeted me and Sara but ignored Kieran.

Kieran winked at me behind his back as we went inside to order.

Kieran had a rum raisin milkshake. Sara had a double chocolate sundae. I

ordered a triple dipped cone. Chris
had a vanilla shake.

I sat down at the picnic table Chris
had been at. Kieran sat beside me,
grinning at Chris's scowl. Sara sat on
the other side across from Kieran, so
Chris sat facing me.

"Delia," said Kieran in a
deliberately casual tone, "what kind of
person traditionally orders a vanilla
milkshake? Are they as boring as I
think they'd be?"

Sara kicked his shin under the
table, but so obviously that we could
all tell she was doing it.

Chris's neck was turning red.

"Don't be a jerk, Kieran." I turned
my back to him and asked Chris,

"What's happening with the fire? Is it getting closer?"

Chris shrugged. The water bombers are keeping it back and trying to push it up the mountain away from town.

Sara smiled at him, "What is your crew doing?"

"We're helping with the firebreak above the point at the moment. The Wildfire Service has heavy equipment clearing a strip of land and the Laketon Fire Department is helping to clear flammable debris out of it."

"Sounds exhausting," Sara said.

Chris nodded, "Yeah. Dirty, hot, and tiring. But it might save Laketon. So I'm glad to be out there doing it."

He looked meaningfully over to Kieran, who developed a slow smirk, but didn't respond to the implied insult.

"A firefighter told me he thought he saw Zuzu up on the forestry service road yesterday."

"What? Zuzu is gone?"

Kieran snickered. "Seriously? You didn't see all the posters? What kind of hopeful boyfriend are you?"

Chris's neck got even brighter red, but he turned from Kieran and looked earnestly at me. "It's so weird she'd go into the forest when most animals are running away from the fires. What happened?"

"She saw something in the forest, jumped our fence, and chased after it.

She's been gone two days now."

"I didn't know. I'm sorry."

His eyes didn't look sorry. He looked like he was glad the demon spawn who defended me wasn't there to stand between us anymore.

Just then, a truck full of fire fighters pulled up. They were still in the gear with hard hats and filthy uniforms. Ash was smeared on their faces.

"Hey, Chris," one said as he went by. "Is this the girl?"

Chris's colour rose from his neck into his face. He sputtered, "Ah, these are friends from school." He pointed at us as he told our names.

"Delia?" said one. "Are you the

WILDFIRE!

one on all the lost poodle posters?"

"Yes. Have you seen her? A firefighter in a truck saw her near a road yesterday."

"I didn't see her myself, but one of the pilots was saying this morning that he thought he saw a skinny white dog run into sight, just as he was making a water drop."

"A water drop." I stared at him as I visualized that. "Wait. Dropping water ON THE FIRE?" My voice had risen several pitches. What was Zuzu doing that near the fire?

~ 8 ~

The firefighters went inside to get their ice cream and I sat eating my double dip cone and pondering.

"Are you okay?" Chris asked.

"Where are the fire lines, now?"

"Pardon?"

"The fire lines. Do you know if Zuzu has crossed the fire line and gone closer to the fires? That doesn't make any sense. Animals know to instinctively move away from fires, don't they? Zuzu isn't stupid."

"I have only seen animals coming out of the fire zone."

"Why would Zuzu go in?" I muttered to myself.

"Do you think she could be protecting something?" asked Sara. "Were poodles bred as livestock guardian dogs or herders?"

"No, they're water retrievers. They were meant to go after ducks and geese shot by hunters, you know, the ones that fall into lakes and ponds. Though Zuzu does like to herd children and will guard our yard against neighbourhood cats."

Sara laughed.

Chris snorted, "Zuzu thinks she's a protection dog. You should see how she snarls when I come near Delia."

"That's just good sense. She reads

danger," Kieran drawled with a smirk to me.

Chris sputtered and would have argued, but Kieran lifted a placating hand. "No, no. I'm just joking. Don't get yourself in a knot."

Kieran looked at me thoughtfully, "What do you think made her jump out of the yard? *Could* she have been trying to protect you from something? There are a lot of predators in the forests."

There was flurry of activity around us as the fire crew found seats around a picnic table. Some of them had more than one dessert. One had a milk shake, a banana split, and a brownie sundae in front of him and was brandishing a spoon with gusto.

Sara glanced at each of us in turn. "Are the animals leaving the woods? Have we seen more wildlife in town?"

I shrugged. "I haven't heard anyone say anything. I haven't seen anything. Have any of you?"

The others shook their heads.

It wasn't uncommon for deer, elk, or bears to wander through town. We were surrounded by forest. We had lots of rules about putting out our garbage, to avoid drawing bears into town on pick-up days.

One of the firefighters leaned over. "There are definitely more animals moving toward town and the shore of the lake. I was in the helicopter and saw a family of bears coming across the beach access along the highway yesterday and there are lots of deer hovering in beach front property. Now that the highway is closed, it's a bit of a wildlife corridor. There are lots of deer on the move. I suspect most animals try to get through town at night. Certainly the wildcats and deer are most active at dawn and dusk."

I fought the lump that rose in my throat at his news.

"Why do you ask?" he added.

"Her dog is lost," said Kieran, glancing at my face and reading my distress. "She went into the woods Sunday night chasing after something."

"Oh, I'm sorry to hear that," said

the fire fighter. "Just one day is a long time to be out in the woods during a forest fire."

He looked so glum, I knew he thought there was no hope that Zuzu was all right, and I burst into tears.

Kieran put an arm around my shoulder. "Shh. It'll be all right. Zuzu will come back. You'll see."

I closed my eyes and leaned into him. Across the table, I heard Chris harrumph.

This wasn't good. I couldn't just wait here like a ball of goo, waiting to hear Zuzu's fate, or worse, having to look for her charred remains after the fire was out. I sat up straighter. I smiled my thanks at Kieran, who offered a gentle smile.

"Chris," I said, my voice steely with determination. "Who do I talk to about joining the fire department?"

Beside us, the fire crew whooped, and one patted me on the back. "That's the attitude, missy!"

Missy?

Jerk.

"I can take you over to the hall right now," said Chris. The captain is bound to be there. He's really busy coordinating everyone. I'm sure he'd be glad to have you."

Kieran leaned over, his shoulder nudging mine. "Are you sure about this? It's dangerous to fight fires."

I nodded.

Sara took my hand and gave it a squeeze. "I think it's a good idea. You'll be able to talk to more people and see if there are more sightings. The more people looking for Zuzu, the better her chances of being found." She stood up to put her sundae dish into the garbage can. "I'll walk you over, too. Coming Kieran?"

Chris gave Kieran a look of hatred that would have made me laugh under less stressful conditions. I didn't acknowledge I'd seen anything, put my cone wrapper into the garbage, and after dabbing my mouth, tossed my serviette after it.

Kieran stood as well, lobbing his milkshake cup over our heads. It plopped neatly into the garbage. He winked at me. "I have some stuff to do, so I'll head back home." He looked at Sara and added, "See you both by six o'clock for dinner."

Sara glanced at her phone to confirm the time and nodded. "Sounds good. We'll be there."

The three of us started walking toward the fire house by the highway junction. With Sara on my left and Chris on my right, I felt like I had my own honour guard.

If I could get onto a fire crew, I could go into the woods, and I could find Zuzu.

At them meeting, they gave us paperwork to fill out and we got to practice with some of the tools. With all my sizes recorded, they would have official fire safe uniform for me by tomorrow. I just needed to have my own boots. I was thankful I'd thought to take Brian's old ones.

I took my papers off to the bathroom, and sitting on the toilet, I forged my parents' signatures. What they didn't know wouldn't hurt them.

I couldn't just sit around waiting for bad news. There'd been two sightings. I knew where to look. I had to get out there and rescue Zuzu from whatever situation she'd gotten herself into. I would find Zuzu.

I would.

Zuzu had to be okay.

She just had to be.

What would I do if I lost the only thing in the world who loved me unconditionally?

~ 9 ~

Thursday night we'd stayed up late and walked down to the lake shore. Along with a lot of Laketon families, we sat silently on the benches, logs, and rocks watching the vivid swaths of red and orange throbbing like luminous lava in the hills. The stars were gone. The moon glowed an ominous red. We coughed at the acrid bite of the smoke, but stayed anyway, mesmerized by the sight of the menace in the hills above town. We sat vigil, sending our thoughts or prayers to the sky to whatever deity might protect our homes and the firefighters.

The next morning the smoke was so thick we could see wisps floating in the road in front of the house. The world appeared in soft focus. Ash covered everything. There were little flecks of grey, like nail clippings on the deck chairs. These ashen evergreen needles dissolved to powder when we brushed them off.

The water bombing planes and helicopters were out.

"It's like living in Armageddon," Sara said, sipping her iced coffee as we sat on their back deck and looked at the billows of smoke in the hill. The air had a brown tinge. It was like looking at sepia toned photos.

"It's getting closer isn't it?" I whispered to Sara. "My neighbourhood is going to be the first to burn."

"Don't say that. Look how hard the crews are working! Remember what Fire Chief Parker said about the retardant and the fire breaks? I think it will work."

Kieran stepped onto the deck with his hands curled around his own coffee. "You only think it will work because you're an optimist. Delia is right to be concerned. It's not looking good."

Sara grunted. She'd picked up her phone and was scrolling. "The forecast says the wind direction is going to change, and the fire is going to be pushed over the mountain away from town," she stuck out her tongue at Kieran, "so there!"

"I'm going to text Brian and see if he knows anything more," I said. What good was having a brother on the fire line if I couldn't wheedle him for information? I sent off a message and waited.

"Is he in cell range? They might not be able to connect up in the hill if any of the cell towers have burnt down."

Sara scowled at him. "Why must you be so negative!"

"I'm just being realistic! Delia needs a rational advisor at a time like this." He glanced over to me. "Let's go in. This smoke is just gross. I'll make you both another ice coffee."

"Thanks," I said, "that'd be nice." I pushed past him and set my cup on the kitchen counter. Then I went into the living room and collapsed on the couch. Movement from the corner of my eye made me do a double take. "Sara! Come here!"

Sara ran over and joined me at the window. "Oh! Gosh!"

"What is it? called Kieran from the kitchen.

"You won't believe it," Sara said, "come see!"

Kieran came in with his hands wrapped in a dish towel. "Oh!"

The three of us sat kneeling on the

couch, arms on the windowsill and watched as three deer stole green apples from a neighbour's tree.

Several rabbits were sitting on various neighbour's lawns, munching.

A large black bear and two cubs almost the same size were strolling down the street.

The deer's ears flicked nervously, but they kept eating until the bears stepped onto the lawn. Then the deer bounded down the road, and the bears all stood on their haunches to investigate the tree.

A tone announced a text message. Brian had replied, "Fire is moving. I'm busy."

Another tone announced a message

from my mom. "How are you?"

I got off the couch and wandered into the kitchen. "Everything's fine," I wrote back. Sara's family are kind hosts. How are you and dad?" I definitely wasn't going to tell them I was volunteering with the Fire Department, or that the fire was moving closer to the town. They worried enough as it was.

My phone rang. Mom wanted to talk. "We're fine," she said. Dad says hello. Have you heard from Brian?"

"Yes. He's busy working. Are Grandma and Grandpa doing okay? Is she out of the hospital now?"

That got her talking. For ten minutes she discussed Grandma's operation and the renovations needed for her house and all the things they were doing to help. There was a crash and she said, "Oh no! The dishes! Talk to you later."

I waited for a 'Love you!' but the phone went silent. I shouldn't have been in the least surprised.

"Holy!" Kieran whispered. "This is bizarre!"

Sara just gasped.

I went back to the window and stared at the massive cougar walking down the road.

"It's like living in a bloody zoo!" Kieran said.

"We shouldn't be surprised. Their home is burning. Where else are they going to go?"

"Isn't it funny," I said, watching the incredible grace of the big cat's muscles rippling, "that yesterday we hadn't noticed any wildlife in town, and today we see this?" The cat was huge.

We watched as it lowered its head and crouched, staring. All that moved was its flicking tail.

"Uh oh," said Kieran. "I think one of those rabbits is about to be dinner."

"I can't look!" said Sara turning as the cougar pounced.

Another tone on my phone made me look away, too.

"Got it!" said Kieran. He hooted with laughter, "Look at the rest of them go!" At least six rabbits were sprinting in all directions.

I glanced down at my phone. Chris had written, "Situation briefing and crew assignments. Fire Hall at nine o'clock. See you there?"

I sent back a thumb's up icon.

I flipped through messages I'd missed, and there was the one from the fire dispatch about the meeting. I looked at the time. I had about forty-five minutes to get to the hall. It was only a ten-minute bike ride, so I had time to grab something to eat.

"I've got a meeting. What's for breakfast?"

Kieran and Sara joined me in a production line to make toast, bacon, eggs, and fresh fruit. I made myself a scrambled egg and bacon toasted sandwich to eat there and put an orange in my pocket for a snack later. "See you guys, later," I said heading toward the door.

"Wait," said Kieran. "You shouldn't go by yourself when there are bears and cougars strolling the streets."

"I am pretty fast on my bike, though."

"Both a bear and a cougar can outrun your bike," Kieran said thoughtfully. "I'll ride with you; I can distract anything wanting to attack you."

"I'll come, too. I have my longboard," Sara added. "And I'll bring the bear spray cannister."

~ 10 ~

The trip to the Fire Hall was
relatively uneventful. We saw deer
down one side street and there was a
bear in the distance down another, but
we didn't see the cougar, and being on
wheels means we were early for the
meeting.

Chief Parker came over to us,
eyeing Kieran and Sara. "New
recruits?"

"No, we were just escorting Delia
to ensure she got here safely. There's
a lot of wildlife in town."

The chief nodded. "Yes, I've been

hearing lots of reports. You saw a bear?"

"Deer, bear, and we saw a cougar nab a rabbit this morning," Kieran explained.

"Really? I hadn't heard any reports about a cougar come into town. Where did you see it? I'll send a report to the Fish and Wildlife Service. I would hate one to get comfortable here. It'd have to be killed. They're too dangerous for little kids and pets."

Pets like Zuzu.

"Sir," I said, "have there been any reports of a dog in the fire zone?"

"Ah, you're the one with the missing standard poodle?"

I nodded.

He looked around the room, "Davis! Come talk to Delia!"

A tall guy, maybe late twenties or early thirties came over. Neither his uniform nor his hands were particularly clean. He had clearly been fighting the fires recently. "Yeah, Chief?"

"Weren't you the one in the helicopter early this morning? Did you see something?"

"Yeah, I thought it was a sheep at first. Then I figured it was one of those curly dogs. Doodle?"

I bristled a bit. "If it was Zuzu, she's got a pedigree full of champions. She's not a mutt like a doodle."

Davis shrugged. "Whatever. Whitish dog. Can't tell more from the air."

"Yeah, sorry." I muttered. "Where was she?"

"Up the forestry service road, in the area where we are going to be starting mop-up today, actually."

"Really?" That was the best news I'd had in days.

"There's a grizzly up that way, too. We have seen it a couple of times moving through the area."

"Oh." That was worse news.

I spotted Chris as he came into the hall.

He waved, then checked his enthusiasm and strolled over to us. "What's up?" he said, all chill.

Ignoring the idea of a grizzly near

town, I flashed a grin at him that made him step back. "Davis spotted Zuzu! We're going to be working in the same area today! Maybe we'll see her!" I turned to the chief. "When can we get up there?"

He put up a hand and laughed. "Don't get ahead of yourself. We need to go over the mop-up procedure, so you know what you're doing. We need to set the crews and make sure everyone knows the safety plan. We're not rushing up a blazing mountain because your dog is up there. Priorities, right? You can't go looking in the woods for a dog when you've got work to do. The mop up zone is the safest place, but during a wildfire, that isn't saying much. It's dangerous work. You're clear on that?"

I must have looked uncertain.

"Listen kid, you're not going up there if you're going to be distracted. The fire has moved up the hill and the area we're looking at for mop-up is safe now, but things can change in an instant. You need to be where we expect you to be in case everyone has to bail out of there quickly. Got it?"

"Yes, sir." This wasn't good news. Of course, it made complete sense, but I needed to get Zuzu back. If I couldn't go hunting for her, I'd just have to hope when she heard her three whistles, she'd come to me as quickly as she was trained to. Three blasts meant race to me. Zuzu would leave whatever she was doing and come to sit in front of me to get a treat. I patted the dehydrated chicken hearts in the little bag in my pocket. They were Zuzu's favourite, the high value treat for after competitions when she needed her greatest focus.

By now, the room was full of people. Some were in gear with steel toed boots and hard-hats. I looked around nervously, in case Brian was one of them.

Sara nudged me, "We'll head off. Call if you need us?"

"Yeah, thanks." I waved to Kieran as they left and focused on the meeting.

Some of the people were the officials from the Wildfire Service who were directing things, but most were members of the Volunteer Fire Department. The majority were young males, but I wasn't the only girl there. Two of the officials from the Wildfire Service were women. They spoke knowledgeably and concisely. One was a helicopter pilot. Three pilots were sharing the helicopter, working in eight-hour shifts around the clock. She explained one was flying, one was eating, and one was sleeping. It sounded exhausting.

They distributed all the gear and divided us into teams of six to eight. We were assigned spots where the crew truck would drop us off. We were to work within sight of one another, so help was there in case of a sudden flare up. We had shovels, forestry rakes, a rakehoe tool called a McLeod for chopping and turning soil, firefighters' axes with a blade on one side and a pick called a mattock on the other, and each crew had a truck with a huge water tank in the box. There were two hoses attached to our tank.

I was nervous and excited. I had said I wanted to fight a fire, and now I was. There was no one around to tell me that I couldn't do it. The chief hadn't even blinked when I handed in my paperwork with the forged signatures. He didn't know my parents

weren't around to sign. I knew under
normal circumstances parents would
have been expected to come to a
meeting. They had gone when Brian
volunteered during his last year of
school, so they knew what was
involved.

If they'd approved Brian, the
captain would expect that they'd
approve me, right?

Honestly, I was counting on the
fact that by the time Mom found out
I'd been in the fire zone, she wouldn't
consider that small detail of parent
permission. She'd probably blame
Brian for not keeping me out of
trouble. What a terrible role-model a
firefighter big brother was. Ha.

I knew there wasn't a hope that she wouldn't find out that I'd joined. Laketon is small. No one has secrets here for long. I just needed this secret to last until I had Zuzu back.

We piled into the crew pick-up and headed up the mountain.

~ 11 ~

It was eery driving up the mountain through the burnt-out area. All the underbrush was gone, and the evergreen forest was now full of blackened poles and stumps.

The smoke from the fire now burning several kilometres away still filled the air. Our boots kicked up ash as we climbed out of the trucks.

We were all wearing heavy pants, hard hats and steel toed boots to protect us from falling trees. Our job was to study the ground for smoking spots where the fire had moved into

the root systems. Puffs of smoke
meant chopping, raking, and shoveling
to get past the organic soil to the
mineral soil, and when we found
whatever roots or mulch was
smouldering, we turned it, raked it, and
then the guy on the hose came by to
spray it. Some areas, the ground was
still green, but the fire had travelled
along the crown of the trees. That
was strange, too.

Perhaps the strangest thing was
the silence. Usually when Zuzu and I
were walking in the woods, it was full
of rustlings in the underbrush, the
chittering of squirrels, and the songs
and squawks of birds. Now it was
cracking and crunching, and the noise

of the fire crew. It was like being on another planet.

Chris was in my crew. Our crew boss was Davis.

As our crew spread out with their chosen tools, combing the ground for signs of hot spots, I looked around for signs of Zuzu, perhaps tufts of curly white hair caught on brambles or something. I didn't notice anything. "Davis?"

"Yeah?"

"Before I get to work, is it okay for me to whistle for my dog? Just in case she's around somewhere?"

He waved an arm, "Knock yourself out!"

The ash was thick, and puffs of

smoke rose with every step. I coughed and my eyes burned, but I pursed my lips and whistled the three blasts that was the special signal for Zuzu to come running. "ZUZU!" I called as loudly as I could, and I whistled another three blasts before I was overcome with coughing again.

The other guys on the crew looked around, everyone pausing to listen, but there was nothing to indicate Zuzu was out there anywhere.

"Sorry kid," said Davis with a shake of his head. "Let's get to work now. You can try again later."

"Thanks for letting me try."

Davis assigned me to a guy called Aaron, to learn how to use my

Macleod.

Aaron showed me how to chop the ground with the sharp hoe side, then flip it to the rake side with its six fat finger-length tines. I could already tell I was going to have horrible blisters under my gloves tonight.

The crew spread out, raking, chopping. I got into the rhythm, scarcely looking up from the ground. Aaron and I together flipped over a smoking stump. A blaze burst out of it.

My heart thudded in my throat and I yelped.

"It's okay, kid. We'll get it. Come on. Kyle! Hose!"

Aaron chopped with the mattock

side of his axe. I pulled away the pieces he broke off with my Macleod, raking and chopping. Kyle sprayed it down.

When Aaron slipped off his glove to test the temperature of the ground was satisfactorily cool, I slipped off mine, and reached into my waist pack for a water bottle.

I looked around for the rest of the crew. They were spread wide apart working in pairs. I couldn't see Chris or Davis, though.

I took another sip and then paused.

"Aaron? Do you hear something?"

Aaron listened.

There was the drone of the skimmer planes and the thump of

helicopter blades overhead, on their way to drop water on the active part of the fire. There was a truck engine grumbling up the mountain. There was crackle of dried forest. "What?"

There was a high-pitched hiss.

"That," I whispered, my mouth suddenly dry.

There was barking.

"ZUZU!" I shouted, as I dropped my water bottle, grabbed my Macleod and tore up the hill toward the sound.

"Hey, kid! Wait!" Aaron called.

Then there was a scream.

~ 12 ~

I ran through the forest as Aaron hollered behind me. I didn't hear what he said. Obviously, I could guess that he wanted me to come back, but I wasn't going to stop, not when that barking had to be Zuzu, and it sounded like she was in trouble. My first duty was to my dog.

"Zuzu!" I shouted as I ran. "Zuzu, I'm coming!"

I tried to whistle, but I was breathing too hard to make any sounds. With every step puffs of ash rose around me, tickling my nostrils.

Finally, I came up against a bare rock face. I had to stop to sneeze and cough.

"Zuzu!" I called. My voice echoed back from the cliff.

I looked around the blackened stumps and the sparse patches of undergrowth trying to get my bearings. I stood still, straining my ears for the sounds I'd heard. Hisses. Barks. A scream.

There was crackling

In the distance I could hear a rumble. Was it growling?

No.

It was one of the water bombers on its way to the active fire line.

I stood there, panting and realized

that having outrun Aaron and the crew, I was now alone in the forest.

Being with lots of other people in the forest gives security. Animals don't attack large noisy groups of humans.

I couldn't hear the rest of my fire crew.

I couldn't hear Zuzu's barks.

I couldn't hear whoever had screamed.

I couldn't hear birds.

Silence in a forest is bad.

Silence means something is lurking.

I stood absolutely still and felt like an idiot. I had just guaranteed that I'd never be allowed to be part of the

Volunteer Fire Department when this was all over.

I had just increased the odds that some desperate animal would attack me.

The hair on the back of my neck rose and I knew my odds were running out.

I raised my McLeod tool and pivoted in a slow circle, trying to remember everything I'd heard about surviving wild animal attacks:

Play dead with a grizzly, but fight a black bear.

Make yourself as big and tall as possible, and maintain eye contact with a wolf as you back away.

Be big and arm yourself against a

cougar, giving it an escape route. Be ready to show teeth and sound ferocious if it attacks. Be prepared to fight for your life.

My heart was racing like a drum solo. *Stay calm, Delia,* I told myself. *Figure out what it is.*

I inhaled a deep breath as I scanned the blackened stumps and lumpy ground searching for the predator that I could feel was eyeing me.

There was a commotion behind me, and I raised my McLeod, spinning to face whatever was as I let out the best martial arts intimidation shout that I could manage, "YAAAAA!!!"

Chris stumbled into view, panting. "Delia!"

I stared at him, blinking with relief.

"What happened?" he gasped, bent over puffing from exertion, his hands grabbing at his knees. "Why did you scream?"

I shook my head, "I wasn't screaming."

"Then what was?" He didn't sound like he believed me.

"I don't know, but something is here. Can't you feel it?"

He shook his head, still bent over trying to catch his breath.

And then a rattle of pebbles behind me made me glance over my shoulder.

A blur of tawny brown as a huge cougar leapt from the rocks stretching right over me in a huge arc, its claws outstretched toward Chris.

Now I DID scream. I shouted, "DUCK CHRIS!" as I ran forward with my McLeod raised. I was ready to swing at the cat like I was batting a ball to the outfield, but before I could get the rakehoe in motion, a snarling grey and black thing leapt over my head from the same rock the cougar had jumped from.

This is just not fair! I thought. A *cougar AND a wolf?!*

There was no time for Chris to do anything except drop to the ground and curl himself into a ball. He wrapped his hands in their thick leather gloves over the back of his neck beneath the brim of his hardhat.

His tool belt protected his lower back. The grey wolf had its jaws on the cougar's neck as the animals snarled and writhed together.

The wolf's coat was strange, kind of curly. Its tail was an odd shape.

It wasn't a wolf.

It was Zuzu.

The animals twisted and the cougar was on top

I swung the McLeod, shouting curse words that would have got me grounded for a month.

Chris rolled away from the snarling animals.

My McLeod clanged on a rock beside them.

The cougar shook itself with a

hissing snarl, and Zuzu released her grip, still growling.

I roared, "LEAVE MY DOG ALONE!" and lunged at the wild cat, slashing the McLeod back and forth ahead of me.

The cat flashed a look of absolute fury at me as I brought the McLeod down again, its sharp hoe edge slicing into the ground.

The cat's gold eyes stared at me.

Before I could lift the rakehoe up again, Aaron and the rest of the crew burst into our midst.

I shouted, "Watch out!"

Aaron spread his arms wide and started yelling, "BAD KITTY!" in a bellowing voice that probably carried into town.

The cougar's gaze darted frantically around at everyone, and then with another huge leap, it raced off up the mountain.

There was a dark streak as Zuzu went to follow it.

I whistled a blast louder than I had ever managed before. "STOP ZUZU!" I shouted with all the authority I could muster. " Come!"

And Zuzu spun around like it was a tight turn in agility class and she leapt into my arms.

~ 13 ~

I was lying on the ground laughing and squirming while I tried to avoid Zuzu's tongue as she covered me with kisses. "Good girl, Zuzu. Good girl." Forty-five pounds of flying poodle had flattened me, but I didn't care. My grin was so wide it hurt my face.

I wrenched myself up, rummaging in my pocket for the bag of dehydrated chicken heart. "What a good girl you are, Zuzu."

She gobbled the treats and sat in front of me, her tail moving so fast it was just a blur. Her coat was black from the ashes and rubbing up against blackened trees, but at the back of her neck, where her coat was thickest, there was a white gap.

Chris came up to me as I was probing it. "What happened there?"

"I think the cougar ripped out some of her hair. If she'd been a Labrador or something it would have gotten her neck."

"It just got a mouthful of fur?"

I nodded, tears flooding my eyes. I rummaged in my pack for the collar and leash I'd brought. "Oh, Zuzu! I almost lost you."

"Never mind her, you almost lost ME!" said Chris. "If Zuzu hadn't leapt on that cougar's back, it would have killed me!" He shivered.

"Come on, everyone," called Aaron. "Is everyone all right? Chris? Did it get you?"

Chris straightened and looked his body up and down. He stretched his gloved arms forward and rotated them. "I don't feel... Oh. Ow."

There was a long line of red dripping down his shirt from a gash across his left bicep.

"Back to the truck everybody," said Aaron. "We need to get some first aid on that arm. Looks like you're going to need stitches, kid." He unclipped his phone and let the rest of the crew take the lead, as he took up the rear, telling whoever was on the other end of his phone that we had an injured crewman after a cougar attack.

As we walked through the forest, Zuzu walked in perfect heel position at my left side, her leash dangling in a gentle arc in front of me as I held it looped around my right wrist. She kept glancing up to my face, just like we were in a Rally Obedience trial.

"Yes!" I said, as I popped a piece of chicken heart into her mouth.

Zuzu wagged her tail.

Chris walked along beside us. "She's not growling at me anymore."

"I guess having saved you from a wildcat, she's decided she'll tolerate you."

"Good girl, Zuzu," he said, reaching

out to pat her on the head.

Zuzu let out a faint rumble at the back of her throat, then glanced up at me and wagged her tail.

When we got back to the truck, everyone pulled out water bottles and sipped, while Aaron got out the first aid kit. He called Chris over and poured a bottle of water over the gash.

Chris winced as the pink water puddled at his feet and dripped on his boots.

Aaron wrapped some gauze around Chris's arm and observed, "That could have been a lot worse."

"I know." Chris shuddered. "That

was the most terrifying experience of my life."

"You were saved by a poodle, dude."

I stepped forward to hand Aaron a piece of medical tape to secure the gauze. "He was saved by one of the most intelligent members of canis domesticus," I rubbed Zuzu's back. "Consider yourself lucky, Chris."

"Considering how much she disliked me, I am surprised she didn't just let the cougar have me."

"Maybe she considers you family. She's allowed to fight with you, but no one else is?"

Chris laughed as a Wildfire Service truck rumbled up and stopped.

My heart dropped when my brother Brian stepped out of the cab. I turned my back to him. I reached into my pocket and pulled a mask over my mouth and nose. Covered with ash and masked, perhaps he wouldn't recognize me.

"You called in a cougar attack?" asked Brian as he strolled over to us.

Aaron nodded, "Relatively minor injury. It just got one good slash at him. A few stitches and he'll be fine.

"Lucky."

Brian glanced around the crew.

Beside me, Zuzu gave the happy whimper she had for greeting family and thumped her tail against my thigh.

"Zuzu?" Brian said, whirling to look

at her. "Is that you?"

Zuzu's tail thumped harder.

"Oh, wow. Is Delia ever going to be happy to see you!"

"Delia's the one who found her!" interjected Chris before I could give him a warning glare.

Brian's brows dropped. "What do you mean?"

Aaron pointed, "That's Delia."

"What?" Brian roared.

Sheepishly, I pulled the mask down. "Hey."

Brian put his hands on his hips and glared at me. "You have some serious explaining to do young lady!" He sounded so exactly like our mother than I couldn't help bursting out laughing.

He narrowed his eyes even more. "Well?"

Before I could say anything, the claxon wail of an alarm blasted from my phone, and those of everyone else in the crew. It was the Emergency Alert notice.

~ 14 ~

Everyone pulled out a phone to read the announcement. I glanced around to see if there was more smoke coming from somewhere. Over my head the helicopter with its giant dangling orange bucket was flying up to the fire line.

I read the message: "The Evacuation Order for southeast Laketon is rescinded. Residents may return to their homes but should remain on Evacuation Alert at this time."

Chris whooped and punched the air.

Everyone began high fiving and cheering. Grinning ash blackened faces contrasted with their sparkling white teeth.

Our mop up block was finished for the day, so we piled into the pick-ups to head down the mountain.

"Delia!" called Brian, "You and Zuzu come with me."

"I want to stay with my crew!" I called back, over the heads of Aaron and Chris.

Aaron shook his head, "You might as well go get it over with. It's not a long drive back to town. If you don't show up, we'll send a search party."

I rolled my eyes. "Thanks a lot. This is my punishment for running off to find Zuzu, isn't it?"

Aaron laughed, "Might be. Let your brother have his say. We'll meet you for debrief at the hall."

Zuzu happily hopped up into the truck and sat looking out the window, her tongue lolling happily. She was absolutely filthy. I wondered how much shampoo it was going to take to return her coat to its usual white. I might have to shave out the traditional hair style that had saved her life today. I wrapped an arm around her shoulders and gave her a squeeze. "Love you, Zuzu."

She lapped a doggy kiss across my chin, as if to say, "I love you, too."

Brian didn't speak as he waited for

all the crew trucks to pull out and start down the forestry service road. Once we were all moving, he said, "Care to explain what you're doing up here with a fire crew? I know Mom and Dad didn't give you permission."

"I had to find Zuzu. Pilots kept spotting her. I knew if I could get up there..." my voice trailed off.

Brian shifted gears. The truck bounced over ruts and rocks. "Wildfire fighting is not a pink job."

"Don't just parrot Mom and Dad. Think for yourself. You know women can fight wildfires. There are women on your crew. You know they are great at the job."

"Delia. They're not you."

"Fine. Then wildfire fighting is a pink job, because I did it. Jobs I do, are pink jobs, right? You should try mopping every floor in our house every weekend. It's much more work than mopping up forest fires." Which wasn't strictly true, but it was certainly a tedious chore without any glory.

Brian rolled his eyes, so he took my point. "You could have been hurt, and then what would Mom and Dad have said to me? I would have been in so much trouble for encouraging you."

I scoffed. "You never did anything remotely encouraging."

"They're going to say it's not women's work, Delia."

"Look, in just one day I worked with the mop-up crew. I put out flare-ups. I found my dog. I defended a friend from a cougar." My voice was getting louder with every sentence. "I'm not a total screw up. In fact, I am practically a superhero!"

Brian sighed as we pulled into the Fire Hall parking lot. "Fine. I get it. You are capable of fighting fires."

"Thank you." I got out of the cab, Zuzu's leash looped over my wrist. She stood panting happily beside me as Brian joined us, as if she hadn't just put me through a week of torture while she played in the forest.

Brian threw an arm over my shoulder as we walked into the

building. "It's a big brother's job to look after his little sister. I don't want to be a bad brother."

I wrapped my arm around his waist and gave it a squeeze. "I love you, too."

He laughed and squeezed my shoulders.

The other crews were back, too, waiting for the day's debrief. Everyone looked weary from the hard work, but I started to see folks looking at me, and then murmuring. I looked around for Chris. He was sitting in a chair against the wall, talking earnestly.

Chief Parker went to the

microphone and everyone turned to listen. He repeated the information about the Evacuation Order being rescinded and there were more cheers and high fives around the room.

"We do dangerous work," he said, expression grim, and we have to be prepared for the unexpected, but there was a first today in my career fighting fires in town or forest. Young Chris Turlock there was jumped by a cougar today."

There was a gasp in the hall.

"He's lucky to have just received a good scratch. He'll have a manly scar and a good tale to tell in the bar..." he coughed and added, "when he's of legal age, of course."

Folks chuckled.

"In other good news, I know some of you have seen the posters around for Delia's missing dog. We're all thankful that Zuzu went after that cougar, and probably saved Chris's life. So let's hear it for Zuzu!"

The crowd shouted "Hip, hip, hooray!" in an echoing chorus. I blushed. Zuzu wagged her tail.

The chief then carried on with the plans for the next day. I would be on the mop-up crew again, but I was leaving Zuzu at Sara's house. No more bushwhacking for her.

A couple of paramedics came into the hall and went over to Chris.

Zuzu and I eased out of the crowd

and joined them. "How's the arm?"

"Hey," said Chris grinning down at Zuzu. "It's my savior!"

Zuzu wagged her tail.

"I have to go so they can sterilize the wound and I can get stitches now," Chris told Zuzu. "But it'd be a lot worse without your help, girl, so don't think I don't appreciate your efforts."

Zuzu's tail wagged faster.

"Does it hurt?" I asked.

He grunted. "Like a mother."

Zuzu stretched her nose out to him and sniffed his knee.

Chris put out his fist for her to smell.

She pushed her head under his fist so he could scratch her head.

Chris laughed. "Look at that! We're friends now." He smiled over at me. "So, can I take you out for dinner sometime? Or to a dance at the Purple Barn?"

I smiled back but shook my head. "I'm not interested in a romantic relationship Chris, I'm sorry. But like Zuzu, I'm happy to be your friend. Will that do?"

"I'm in the Friend Zone?" He made a melodramatic pout. "Harsh."

"Sorry." I shrugged. "Maybe someday, but not now. I've got other stuff on my mind these days."

Chris stood to follow the paramedics. "Well, at least I tried."

I waved as he headed out the door.

My phone buzzed in my pocket. There was a text from Mom. "Your brother says we should let you join the Volunteer Fire Department."

I typed back, "Yes! Please!"

I smiled over at Brian, who smiled back.

Yeah, it sucked that my parents still needed my brother's endorsement before they trusted that I could do a job traditionally associated with men, but at least it was a start.

Zuzu leaned her back against me. My best friend was home. Laketon was safe. I'd done my part to make it all happen.

It was enough.

I was enough.

Author's Note

The summer of 2021 wildfires raged through the forests of British Columbia. Many of my friends and former students were on Evacuation Order or Evacuation Alert. Those of us in the interior spent weeks glued to the BC Wildfire Service updates, watching the weather, praying for rain.

I wrote this book in eight days under brown, ash-filled skies. I was half-way through the story when I saw a Facebook post about a missing standard poodle in the Monte Lake evacuation area. How astounding it was to see real life was imitating my art! I hope Jenna was eventually found safe, as Delia's Zuzu was.

SLB
Shuswap Lake, BC
August 2021

Acknowledgements

Thanks to Anthony Smith and Ari Hickman for their feedback regarding wildfire fighting strategies, tools, and procedures.

Thanks to the BC Wildfire Service for protecting our communities, for their tools for tracking fires, and the detailed information they post about each Fire of Note, telling how each fire was being fought.

About the Author

Shawn L. Bird (BA, MEd)
is a high school English teacher, an author, and a poet in the beautiful Shuswap region of British Columbia. She is the author of over twenty publications for both teens and adults, including short stories, poetry, novellas, and novels.

In her spare time, she hangs out with her husband, annoys her kids, trains her talented miniature poodle in tricks and agility, plays the harp, and

serves her community with Shuswap
Rotary Club, all while wearing truly
awesome shoes.

Visit her website at
www.shawnbird.com to learn more
about her books, to sign up for her
newsletter for updates about new
publications, or to read original poetry.

Shawn is happy to visit high
school classes, either virtually or in
person, to discuss reading, writing, or
Life in Laketon.

You're invited to write Shawn at
Lintusen Press
PO Box 10019
Salmon Arm BC
Canada V1E 3B9

Here is a sneak peek at the next
Life in Laketon novella.

While I Was Out

"Oh my God, that's Rose! Ethan, help me."

The feminine voice was familiar. I struggled to open my eyes. They were remarkably heavy, as if someone had tied weights on each eye lash. *Whose voice was that?* Faces swirled in my mind as I struggled to match the sound to a vision. A face settled blurrily in my mind. Dark curls. Blue eyes. Who? *Tammi.* I tried to say it out loud, but the sound that came out of my mouth wasn't a word.

They were pulling on me. What were they pulling on? Shoulders. Yes.

Shoulders. That's what they were called. What was missing? Ah. There should be arms, but none seemed to be attached to the shoulders. I thought I should be able to bend... ah...elbows, but couldn't find them. Where were my legs? They were missing, too. I looked down my body. Nothing appeared to be lacking, though I couldn't seem to make any of the limbs I could see actually work. I tried to tell them about that, but there were still no words.

"It's okay, Rose," Tammi murmured. "You'll be fine." Her voice seemed to come from far away. I was cold. The air smelled funny, as if it were purple or maybe orange. *Did smell normally have colour?* Something was strange about that, but I couldn't quite figure out what. The scent was sharp. It hurt my nostrils, like orange and purple blades were slicing from inside my head.

"What do you want to do with her? Maybe we should just ring the door bell and her parents will find her themselves?" That was a male voice. I knew that one, too. What had she called him? *Ethan*. That was it. *Boyfriend*. Her boyfriend. I had a boyfriend. I fought through the spinning fog of images looking for his face. Sandy brown hair. Hazel green eyes. Slight overlap between his front teeth. I felt a tingling sensation like a kiss on my lips. Boyfriend. What was his name again?

There was a pause. "Let's get her inside," Tammi said. Her voice was sharp.

"It's seven in the morning," Ethan said. "Her parents are going to freak at us if we bring her in drunk."

"This doesn't look like drunk to me."

Drunk. I tried to remember drinking. I remembered a bottle of something sweet. Wait. *Seven o'clock in the morning? What?* I tried to ask. *What time is it?* The noises I was making still weren't words, though.

Tammi asked, "What are you trying to say, Rosey?"

I shook my head in frustration, but stopped when it made the swirling images bump painfully together. My stomach churned.

They had found the arms that were attached to me. Through a haze I watched them drape one arm over each of their shoulders. *Where had the arms come from?* They each wrapped a hand around my waist and hauled me up. I could see legs beneath me. I tried to walk, but I couldn't feel the feet actually touching the ground. We got to the back door. My vision had cleared enough to give me a tiny picture framed in fog. *Soft focus.*

"Do you have a key?" Ethan asked.

"No," Tammi shook her head. "Try the door. It might be unlocked if they were expecting her home late."

It was. They hauled me into my family room and dropped me onto the couch.

Ethan stared down at me. "Now what?" he whispered.

Tammi shook her head. "We need to wake up her mom."

Ethan shuddered. "*That* is not going to go well."

"She needs to get to the hospital," she hissed. "Look at her. She's had some drug. Why else was she passed out on the front lawn?"

Ethan stared down at me. His

expression changed. "Oh, shit." He sat down with a thud.

"What?"

Ethan groaned and Tammi frowned at him.

Ethan shook his head.

Tammi smacked him in the shoulder. "What? Ethan! What do you know?"

"Nothing," Ethan said, tightening his lips. "I just heard some guys in the mall talking about this stuff." His eyes were dark and worried. He smelled like scorched onions. How strange. Boys were like onions, I thought. Very complicated. Many layers. And they made you cry. Suddenly crying seemed like an excellent idea, and tears poured from my eyes.

There was a creak above our heads.

"Is someone down there? Rosey, is that you?"

Tammi gulped and called, "It's us, Mr. Dalton. Tammi and Ethan. We have Rose. Something is wrong with her."

WATCH FOR MORE BOOKS ABOUT

LIFE IN LAKETON:

1. Back at You
2. After #8
3. Chancey
4. Wildfire!
5. While I Was Out